Jewel the magical chef makes enchanted dishes,
Giving the kids tasty treats and granting their wishes.

Flying fruit salads soar through the air,
Magical melon and spellbound strawberries everywhere!

Jewel uses magical ingredients on every plate,
That always cures the kids' belly aches.

But a wicked old witch named Marindale lives up the hill,
She switches Jewel's ingredients with nasty, evil meals.

Marindale knows the kids like sweets,
So, she whips up some wicked cupcakes
for the kids to eat.

A dish of green cupcakes lines the round rim,
A dish that has a crusted and rusted old trim.

Colorful frostings dusted with bright sprinkles,
She smiles so very big her one eye wrinkles.

The cupcakes are held high into the air,
And all the kids ate, no cupcakes to spare.

But the curse of the cupcakes soon began,
The kids grew fur and horns from Marindale's evil plan.

Now the colorful frosted cupcake treats,
Had all the kids' faces bumpy like beets.

Luckily, Jewel's magical friends see the witch's spell,
They run to Jewel with a wicked tale to tell.

Jahniyah the cat tells Jewel of the horns and fur,
And Skylar the unicorn reveals the nasty recipe
that was stirred.

Zoe the llama also hears the evil tale that's told,
And the three friends search for magic ingredients
on Unicorn Road.

To save the kids they must help make the cure.
A magical fruit salad from Jewel will work for sure!

They bring bananas, apples, and watermelons for Jewel, She stirs honeydew and strawberries using her magical tool.

With a wave of her wand and a dancing dish,
Spellbound Strawberries and apples will grant their wish.

Jewel finishes her magical dish of enchanted fruits,
The kids eat the delicious treat as Marindale shakes
in her boots.

The fur and horns begin to disappear,
Jewel and her magic friends begin to cheer!

2 Apples,
1 Banana
1 Cup of watermelon diced
4 sliced strawberry
¼ cup Honeydew and Melon
Honey (All Natural)

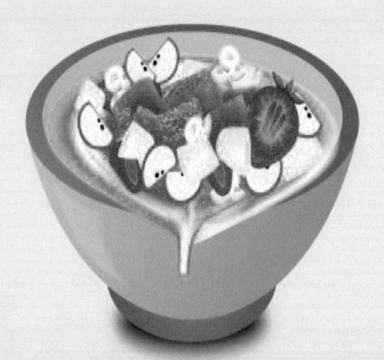

Slice the Apples with an apple slicer

Peel Banana and cut in desired thickness.

Cut open a small watermelon and dice into pieces

Slice Strawberry

Cut honey and Melon dice pieces

Mix all in a bowl

Pour a layer of honey over and enjoy!

Made in the USA
Columbia, SC
09 January 2024

29625016R00015